[redacted]

[redacted]

[redacted]

STAR WARS®

EPISODE III
REVENGE OF THE SITH

VOLUME ONE

ADAPTED FROM THE STORY
AND SCREENPLAY BY
GEORGE LUCAS

SCRIPT
MILES LANE

ART
DOUGLAS WHEATLEY

COLORS
CHRIS CHUCKRY

LETTERING
MICHAEL DAVID THOMAS

COVER ART
DAVE DORMAN

DARK HORSE COMICS

Spotlight

VISIT US AT
www.abdopublishing.com

Reinforced library bound edition published in 2010 by Spotlight, a division of the ABDO Group, 8000 West 78th Street, Edina, Minnesota 55439. Spotlight produces high-quality reinforced library bound editions for schools and libraries. Published by agreement with Dark Horse Comics, Inc., and Lucasfilm Ltd.

Library of Congress Cataloging-in-Publication Data

Lane, Miles.
Star wars, episode III, revenge of the Sith / based on the story and screenplay by George Lucas ; Miles Lane, adaptation ; Doug Wheatley, art ; Chris Chuckry, colors ; Michael David Thomas, letters. -- Reinforced library bound ed.
v. <1-4> cm.
"Dark Horse."
ISBN 978-1-59961-617-9 (volume 1) -- ISBN 978-1-59961-618-6 (volume 2) -- ISBN 978-1-59961-619-3 (volume 3) -- ISBN 978-1-59961-620-9 (volume 4)
I. Lucas, George, 1944- II. Wheatley, Doug. III. Chuckry, Chris. IV. Thomas, Michael David. V. Dark Horse Comics. VI. Star Wars, episode III, revenge of the Sith (Motion picture) VII. Title. VIII. Title: Star wars, episode three, revenge of the Sith. IX. Title: Star wars, episode 3, revenge of the Sith. X. Title: Revenge of the Sith.
PZ7.7.L36Std 2009
741.5'973--dc22

2009002014

All Spotlight books have reinforced library bindings and are manufactured in the United States of America.

War! The Republic is crumbling under attacks by the Separatist leader, Count Dooku. There are heroes on both sides. Evil is everywhere.

In a stunning move, the fiendish droid leader, General Grievous, has swept into the Republic capital and kidnapped Chancellor Palpatine, leader of the Galactic Senate.

As the Separatist Droid Army attempts to flee the besieged Capital with their valuable hostage, two Jedi Knights lead a desperate mission to rescue the captive Chancellor....

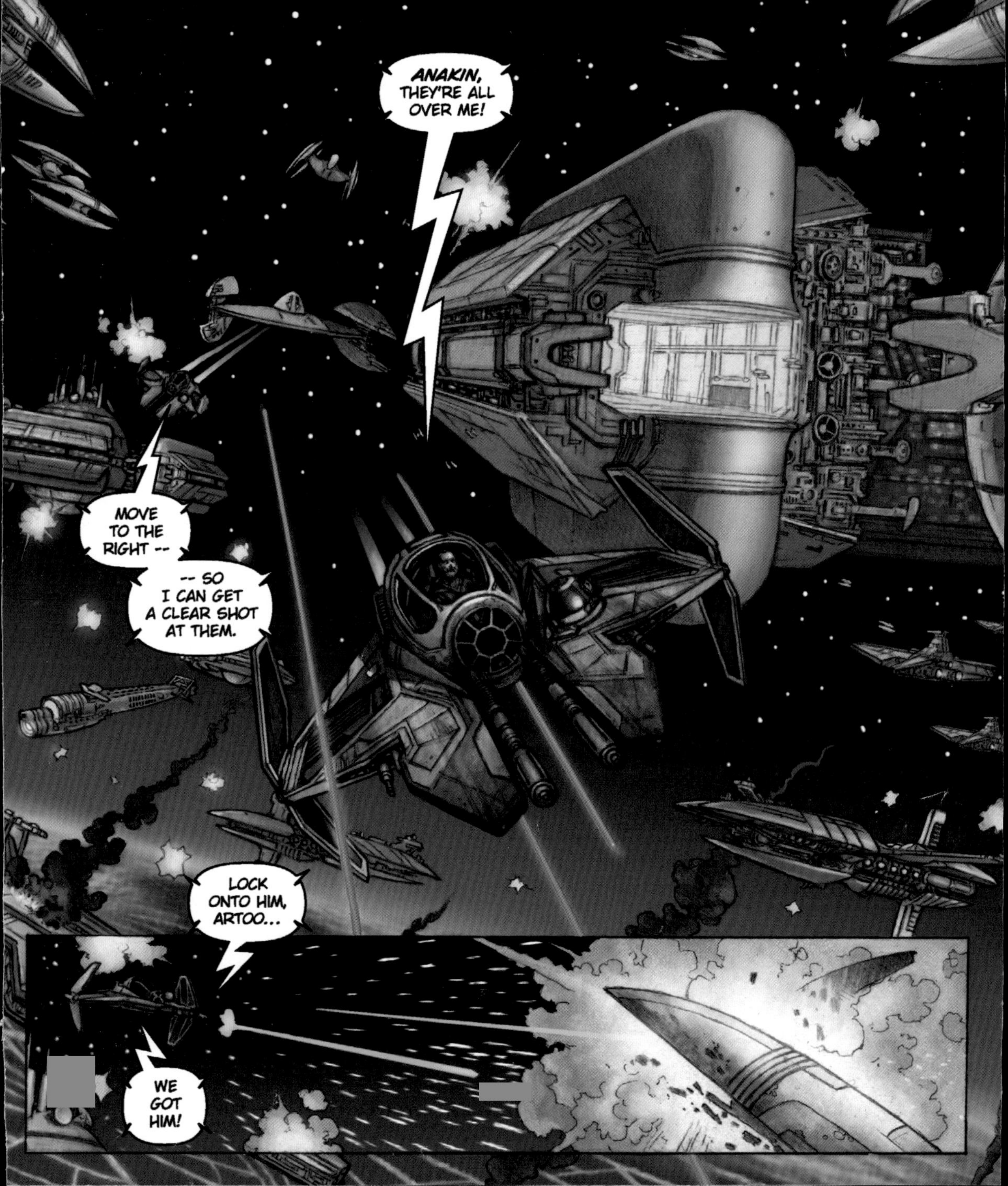

ANAKIN, THEY'RE ALL OVER ME!
MOVE TO THE RIGHT --
-- SO I CAN GET A CLEAR SHOT AT THEM.
LOCK ONTO HIM, ARTOO...
WE GOT HIM!

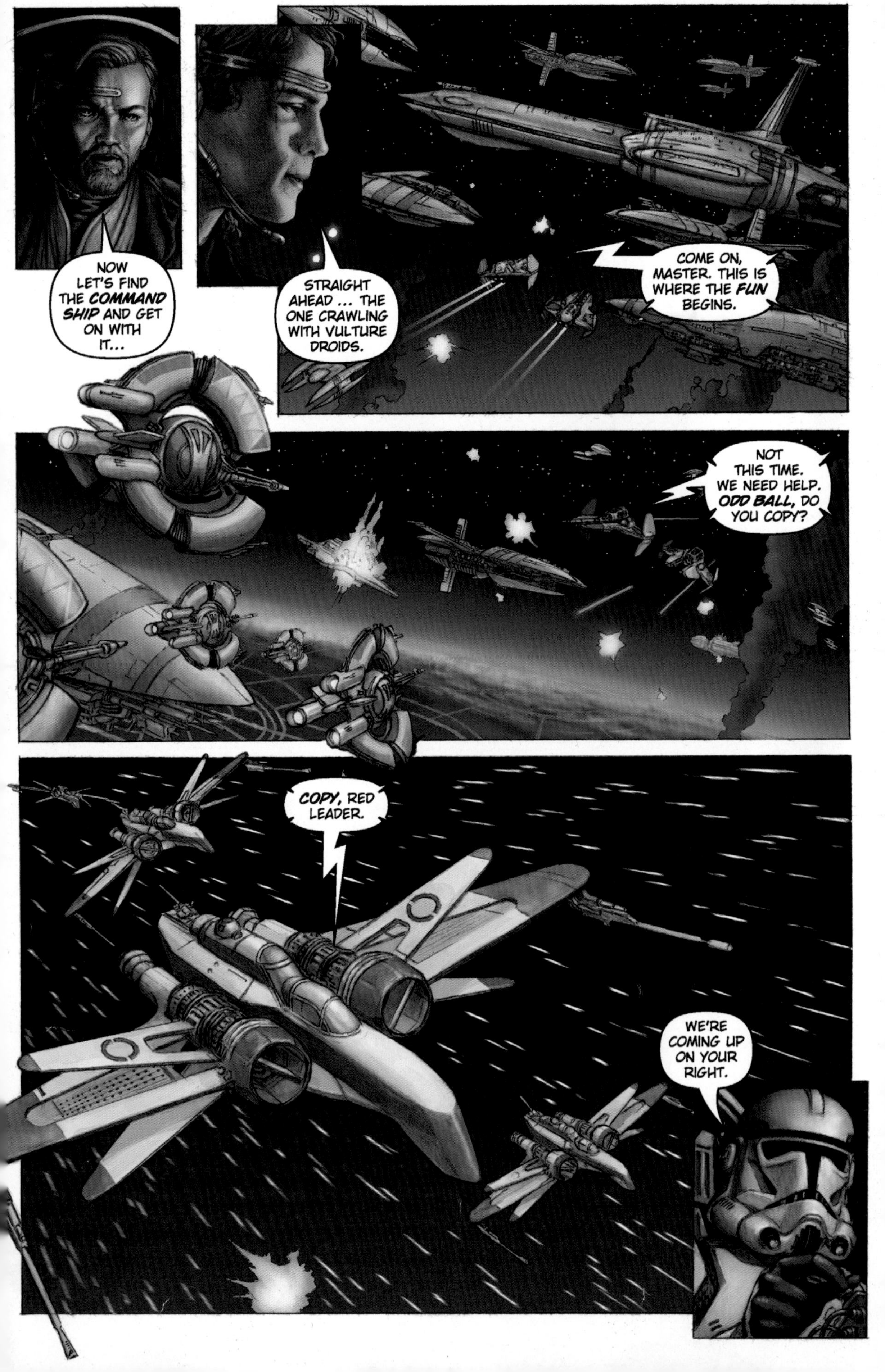
NOW LET'S FIND THE COMMAND SHIP AND GET ON WITH IT...
STRAIGHT AHEAD ... THE ONE CRAWLING WITH VULTURE DROIDS.
COME ON, MASTER. THIS IS WHERE THE FUN BEGINS.
NOT THIS TIME. WE NEED HELP. ODD BALL, DO YOU COPY?
COPY, RED LEADER.
WE'RE COMING UP ON YOUR RIGHT.

THERE ARE TOO MANY OF THEM!

I'M GOING TO HELP THEM OUT!

NO, YOU'RE *NOT!*

THEY'RE DOING THEIR JOB SO WE CAN DO OURS. HEAD FOR THE COMMAND SHIP!

MISSILES!

I'M *HIT!*

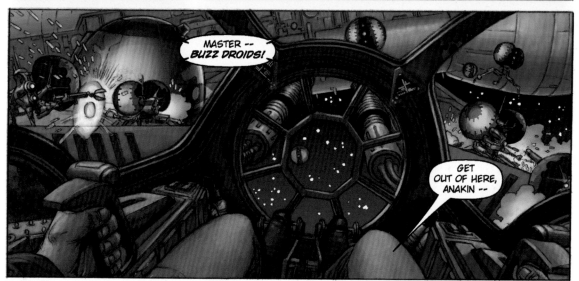

MASTER -- *BUZZ DROIDS!*

GET OUT OF HERE, ANAKIN --

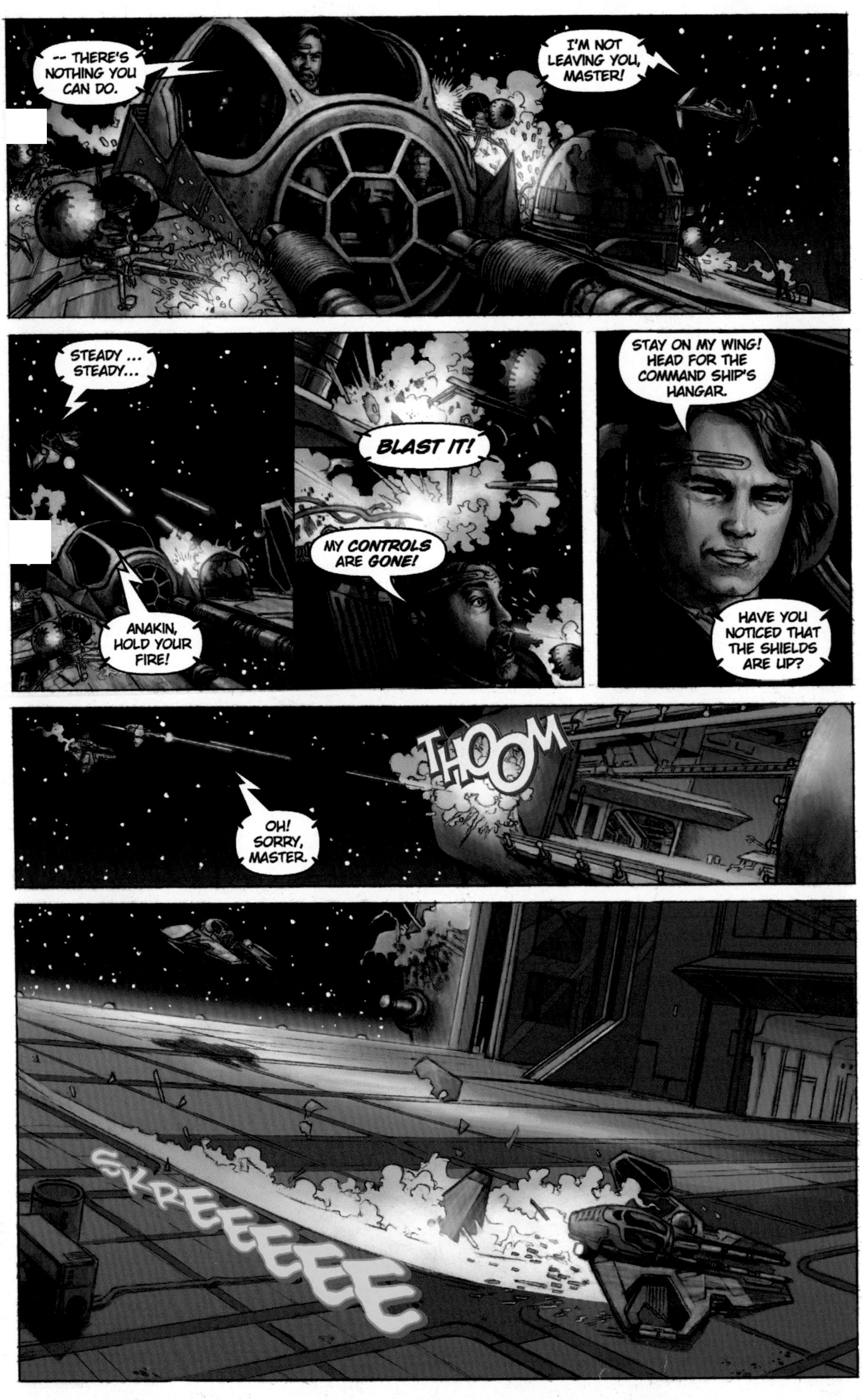
-- THERE'S NOTHING YOU CAN DO.
I'M NOT LEAVING YOU, MASTER!
STEADY ... STEADY...
ANAKIN, HOLD YOUR FIRE!
BLAST IT!
MY CONTROLS ARE GONE!
STAY ON MY WING! HEAD FOR THE COMMAND SHIP'S HANGAR.
HAVE YOU NOTICED THAT THE SHIELDS ARE UP?
THOOM
OH! SORRY, MASTER.
SKREEEEEEE

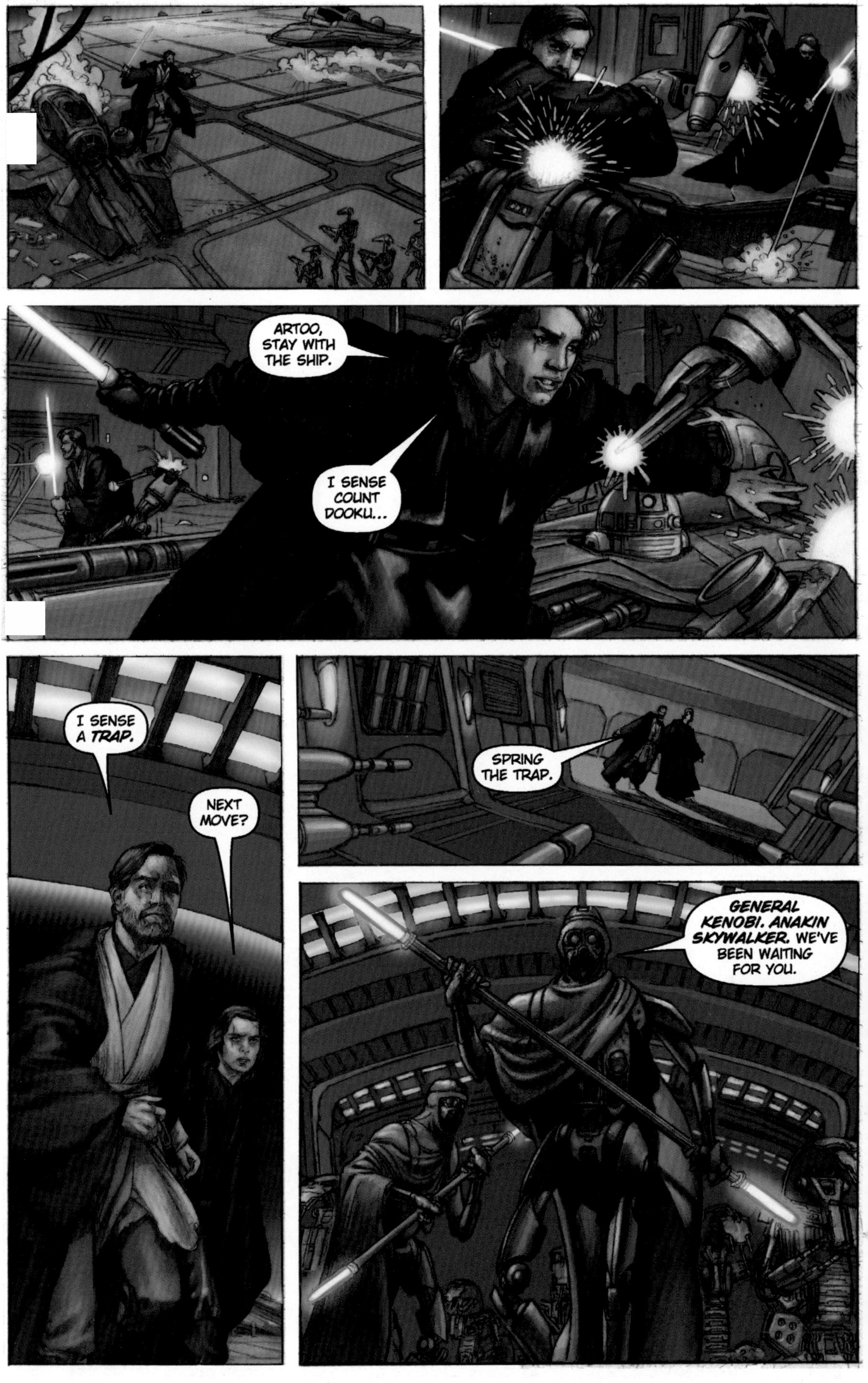
ARTOO, STAY WITH THE SHIP.
I SENSE COUNT DOOKU...
I SENSE A *TRAP.*
NEXT MOVE?
SPRING THE TRAP.
GENERAL KENOBI. ANAKIN SKYWALKER. WE'VE BEEN WAITING FOR YOU.

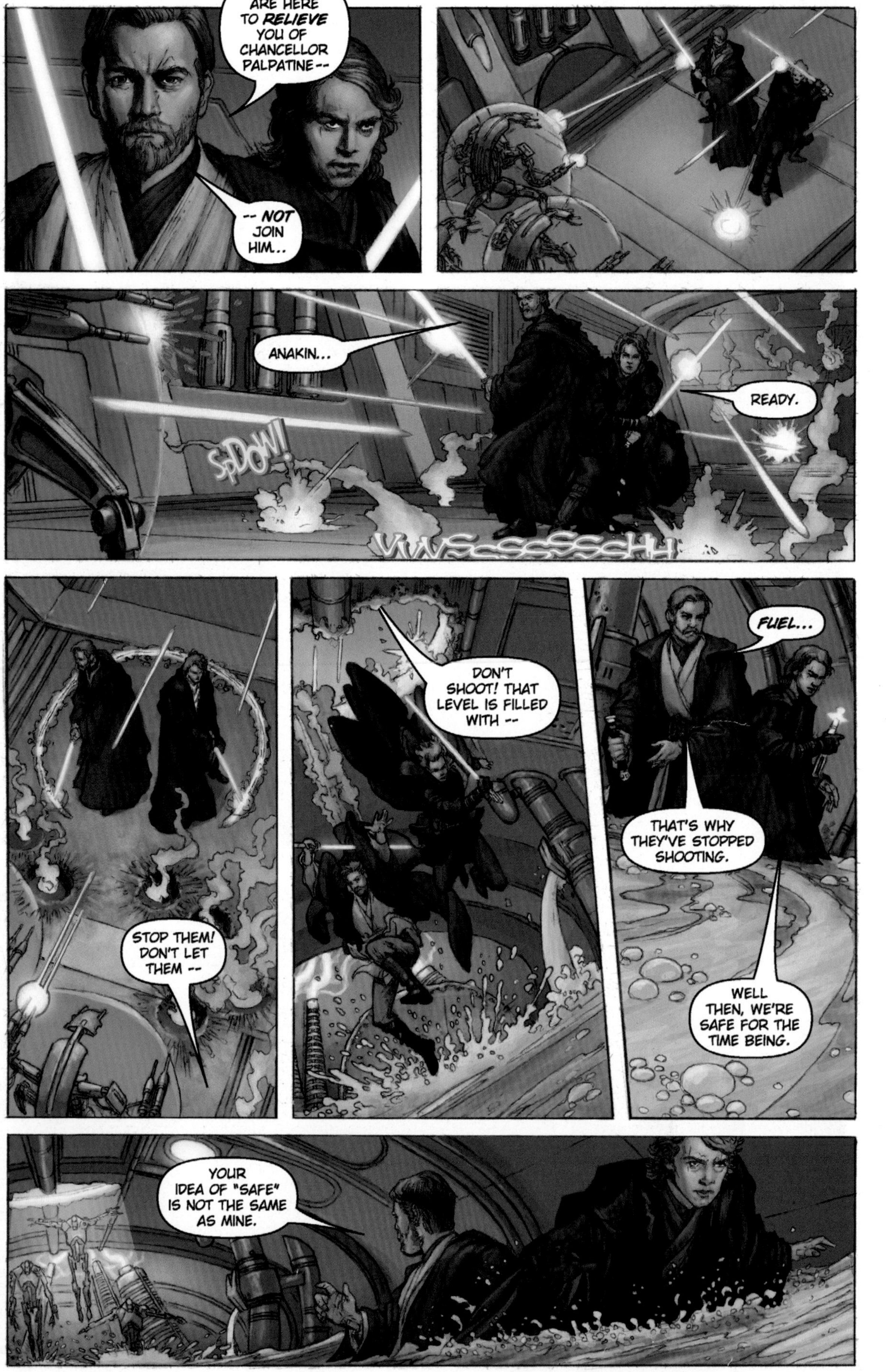
WE ARE HERE TO *RELIEVE* YOU OF CHANCELLOR PALPATINE--
-- *NOT* JOIN HIM...
ANAKIN...
READY.
SPDOW!
VVVSSSSSSCHH
STOP THEM! DON'T LET THEM --
DON'T SHOOT! THAT LEVEL IS FILLED WITH --
FUEL...
THAT'S WHY THEY'VE STOPPED SHOOTING.
WELL THEN, WE'RE SAFE FOR THE TIME BEING.
YOUR IDEA OF "SAFE" IS NOT THE SAME AS MINE.

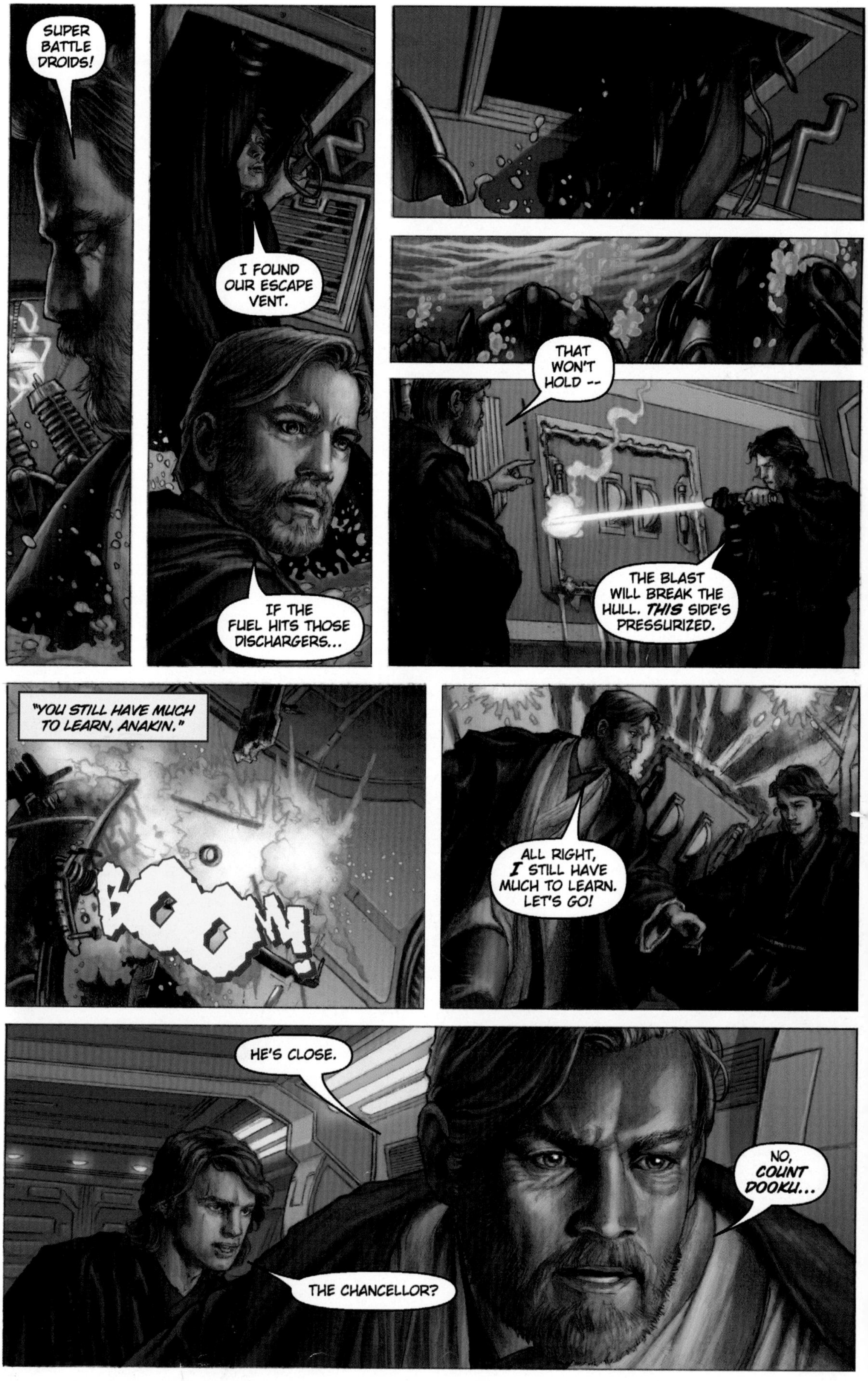
SUPER BATTLE DROIDS!
I FOUND OUR ESCAPE VENT.
IF THE FUEL HITS THOSE DISCHARGERS...
THAT WON'T HOLD --
THE BLAST WILL BREAK THE HULL. *THIS* SIDE'S PRESSURIZED.
"YOU STILL HAVE MUCH TO LEARN, ANAKIN."
BOOM!
ALL RIGHT, *I* STILL HAVE MUCH TO LEARN. LET'S GO!
HE'S CLOSE.
THE CHANCELLOR?
NO, *COUNT DOOKU...*

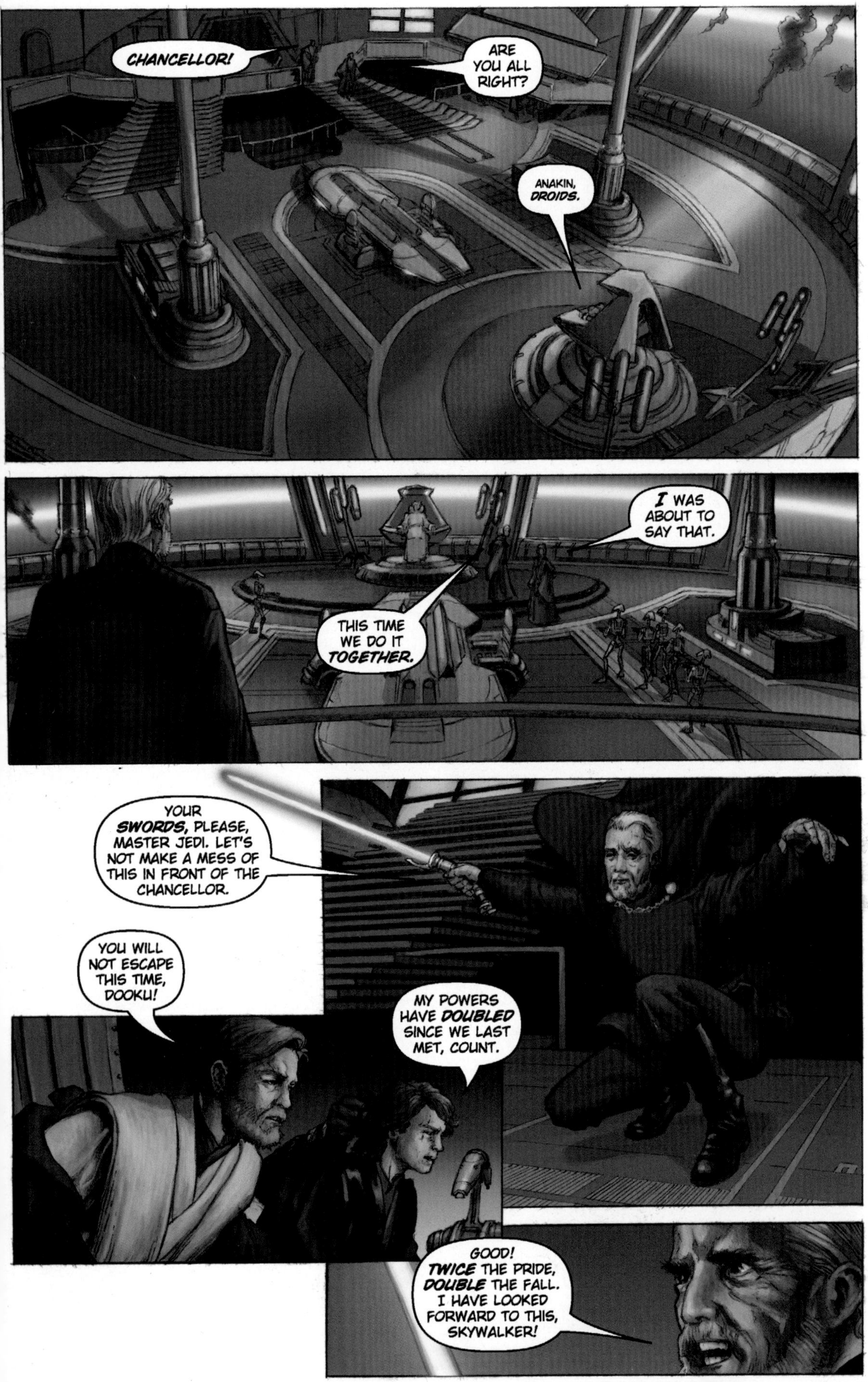
CHANCELLOR!
ARE YOU ALL RIGHT?
ANAKIN, DROIDS.
I WAS ABOUT TO SAY THAT.
THIS TIME WE DO IT TOGETHER.
YOUR SWORDS, PLEASE, MASTER JEDI. LET'S NOT MAKE A MESS OF THIS IN FRONT OF THE CHANCELLOR.
YOU WILL NOT ESCAPE THIS TIME, DOOKU!
MY POWERS HAVE DOUBLED SINCE WE LAST MET, COUNT.
GOOD! TWICE THE PRIDE, DOUBLE THE FALL. I HAVE LOOKED FORWARD TO THIS, SKYWALKER!

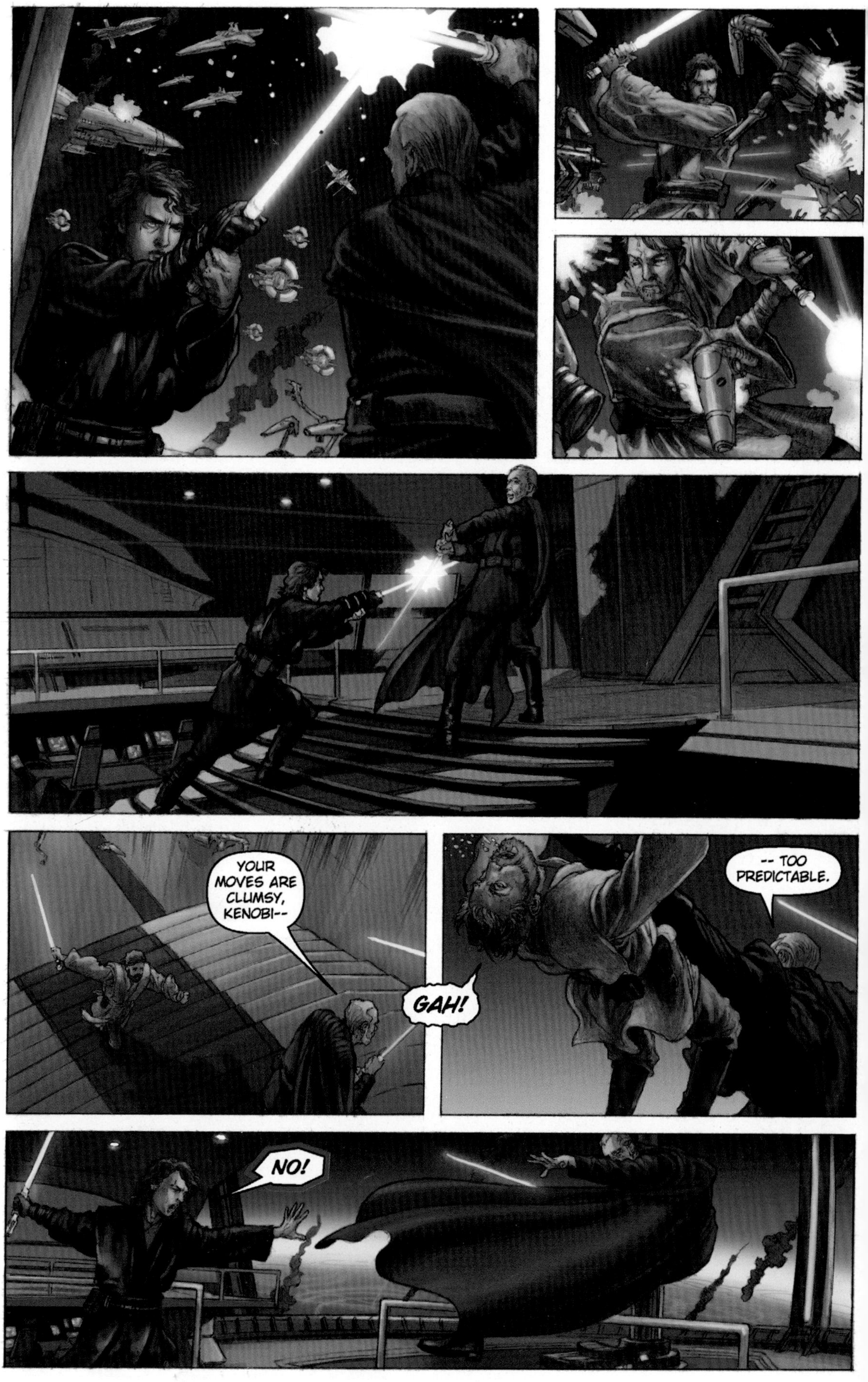
YOUR MOVES ARE CLUMSY, KENOBI--
GAH!
-- TOO PREDICTABLE.
NO!

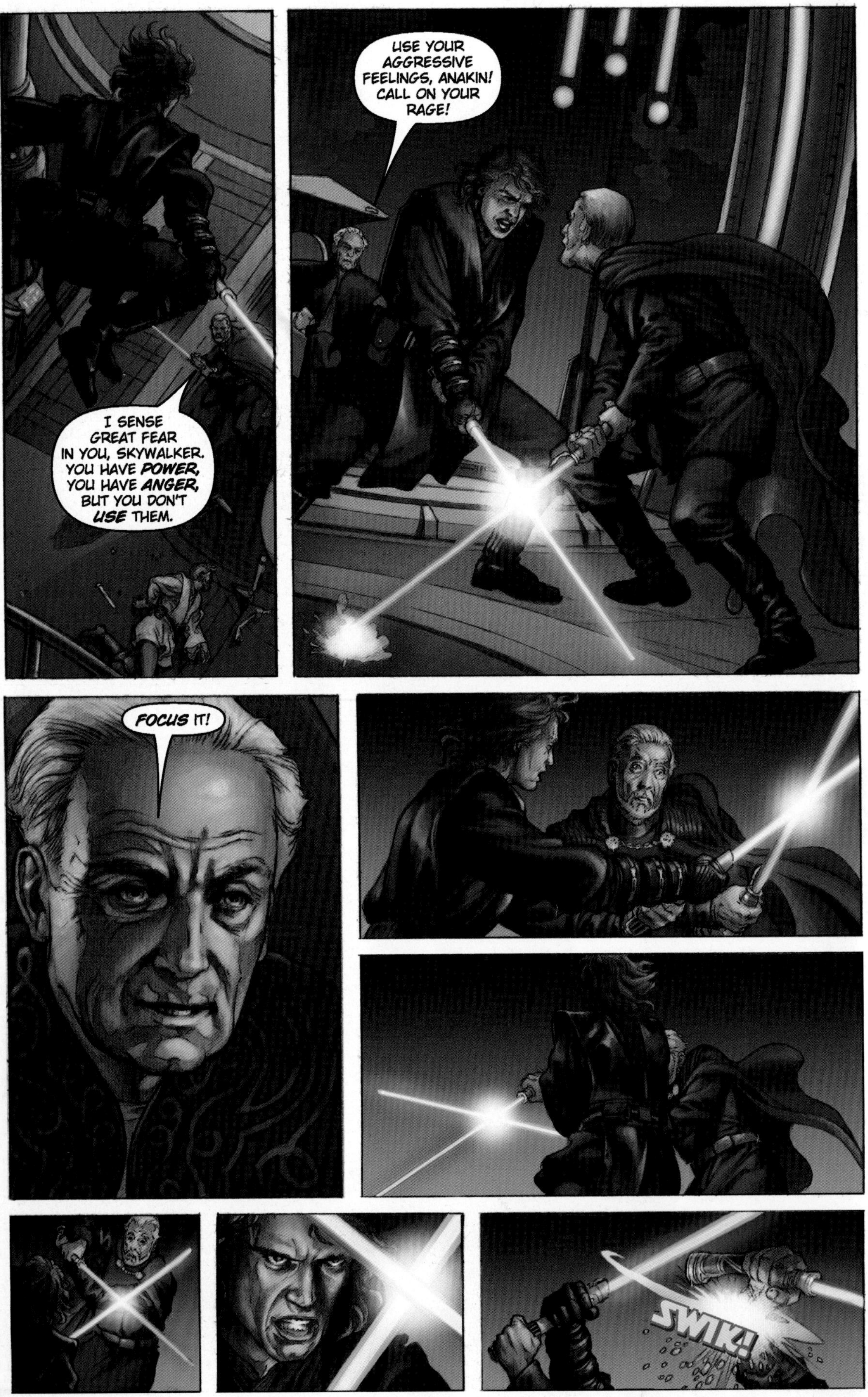
I SENSE GREAT FEAR IN YOU, SKYWALKER. YOU HAVE *POWER*, YOU HAVE *ANGER*, BUT YOU DON'T *USE* THEM.
USE YOUR AGGRESSIVE FEELINGS, ANAKIN! CALL ON YOUR RAGE!
FOCUS IT!
SWIK!

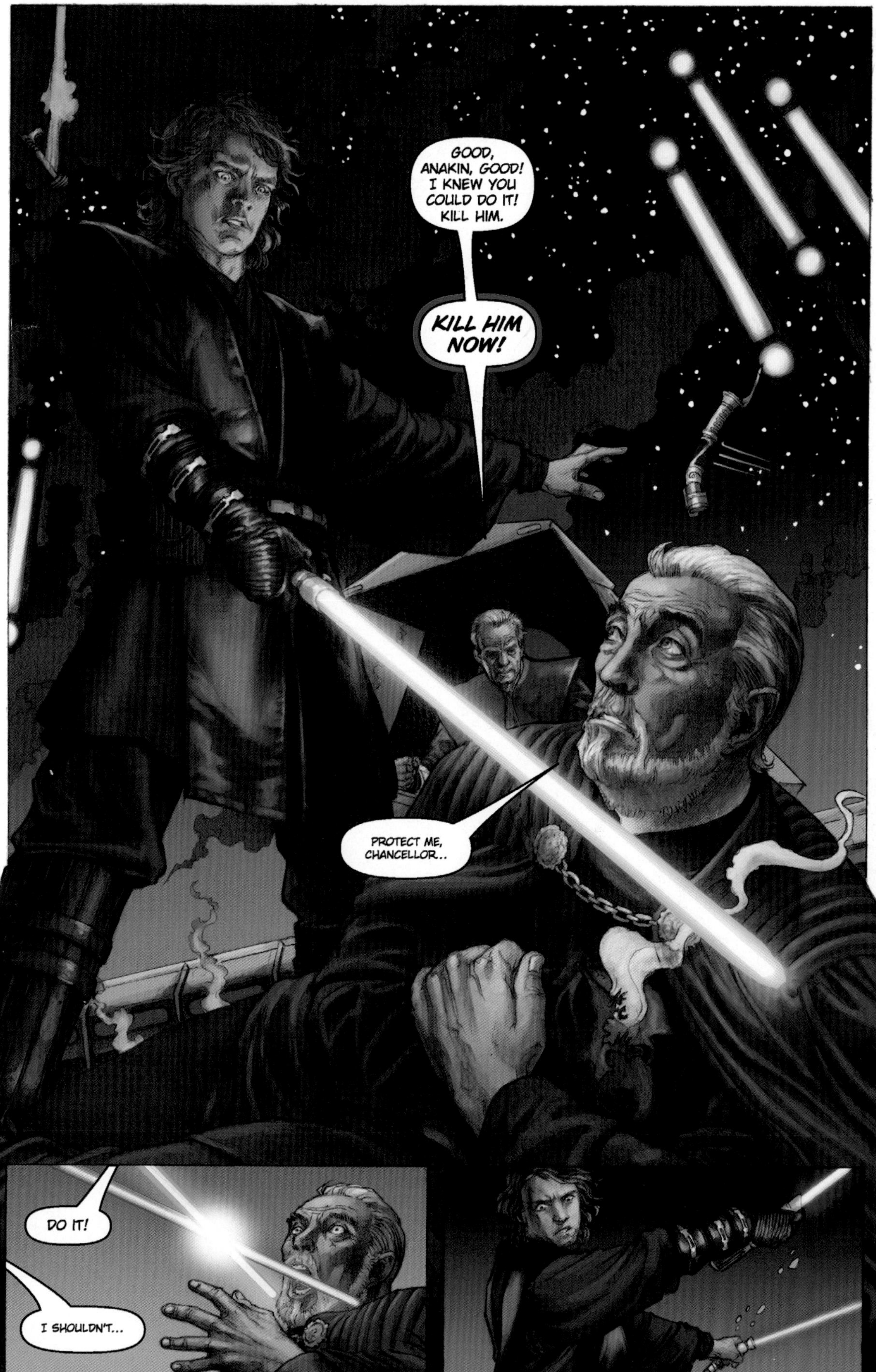
GOOD, ANAKIN, GOOD! I KNEW YOU COULD DO IT! KILL HIM.
KILL HIM NOW!
PROTECT ME, CHANCELLOR...
DO IT!
I SHOULDN'T...

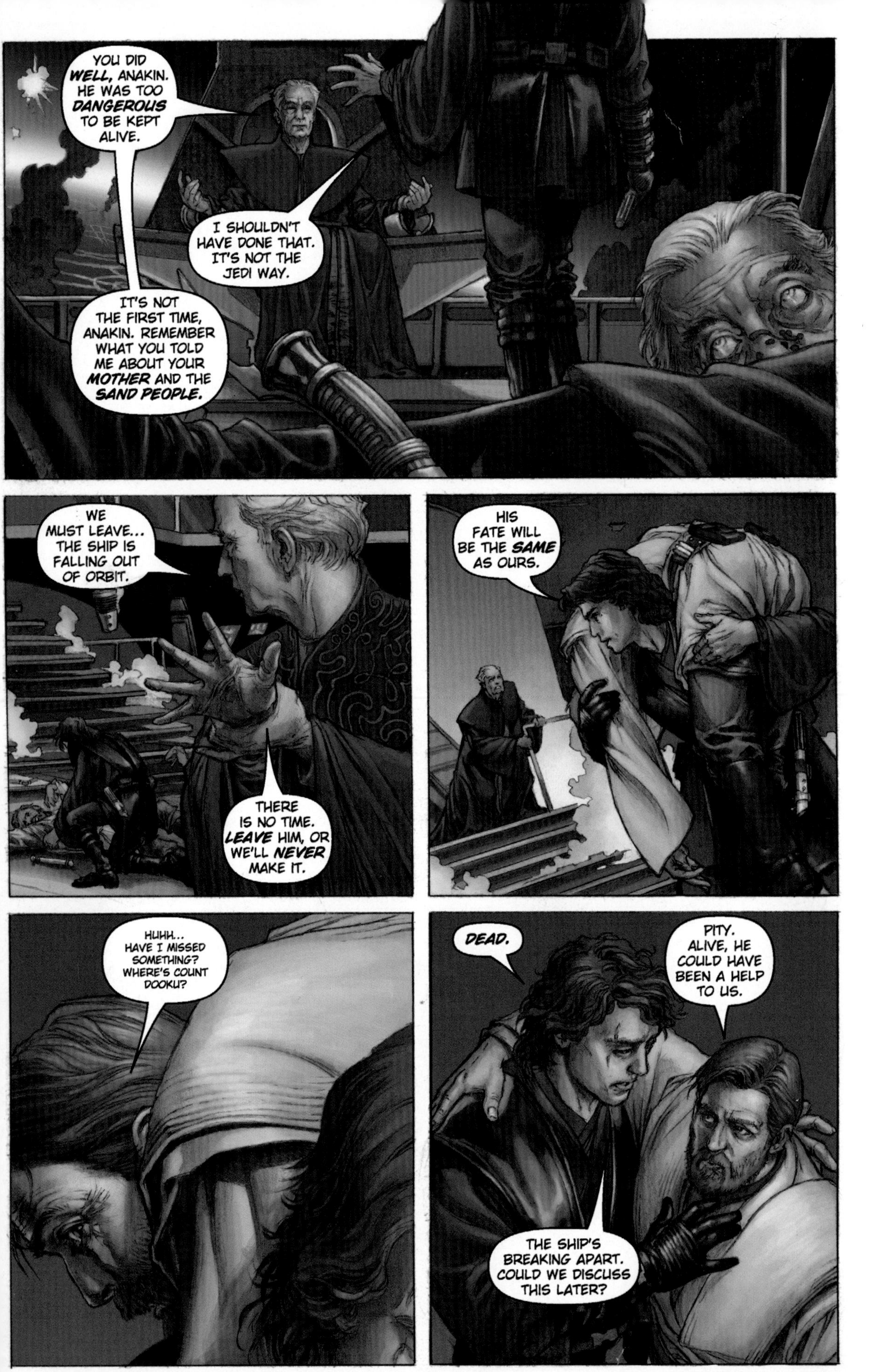

YOU DID WELL, ANAKIN. HE WAS TOO DANGEROUS TO BE KEPT ALIVE.
I SHOULDN'T HAVE DONE THAT. IT'S NOT THE JEDI WAY.
IT'S NOT THE FIRST TIME, ANAKIN. REMEMBER WHAT YOU TOLD ME ABOUT YOUR MOTHER AND THE SAND PEOPLE.
WE MUST LEAVE... THE SHIP IS FALLING OUT OF ORBIT.
THERE IS NO TIME. LEAVE HIM, OR WE'LL NEVER MAKE IT.
HIS FATE WILL BE THE SAME AS OURS.
HUHH... HAVE I MISSED SOMETHING? WHERE'S COUNT DOOKU?
DEAD.
PITY. ALIVE, HE COULD HAVE BEEN A HELP TO US.
THE SHIP'S BREAKING APART. COULD WE DISCUSS THIS LATER?

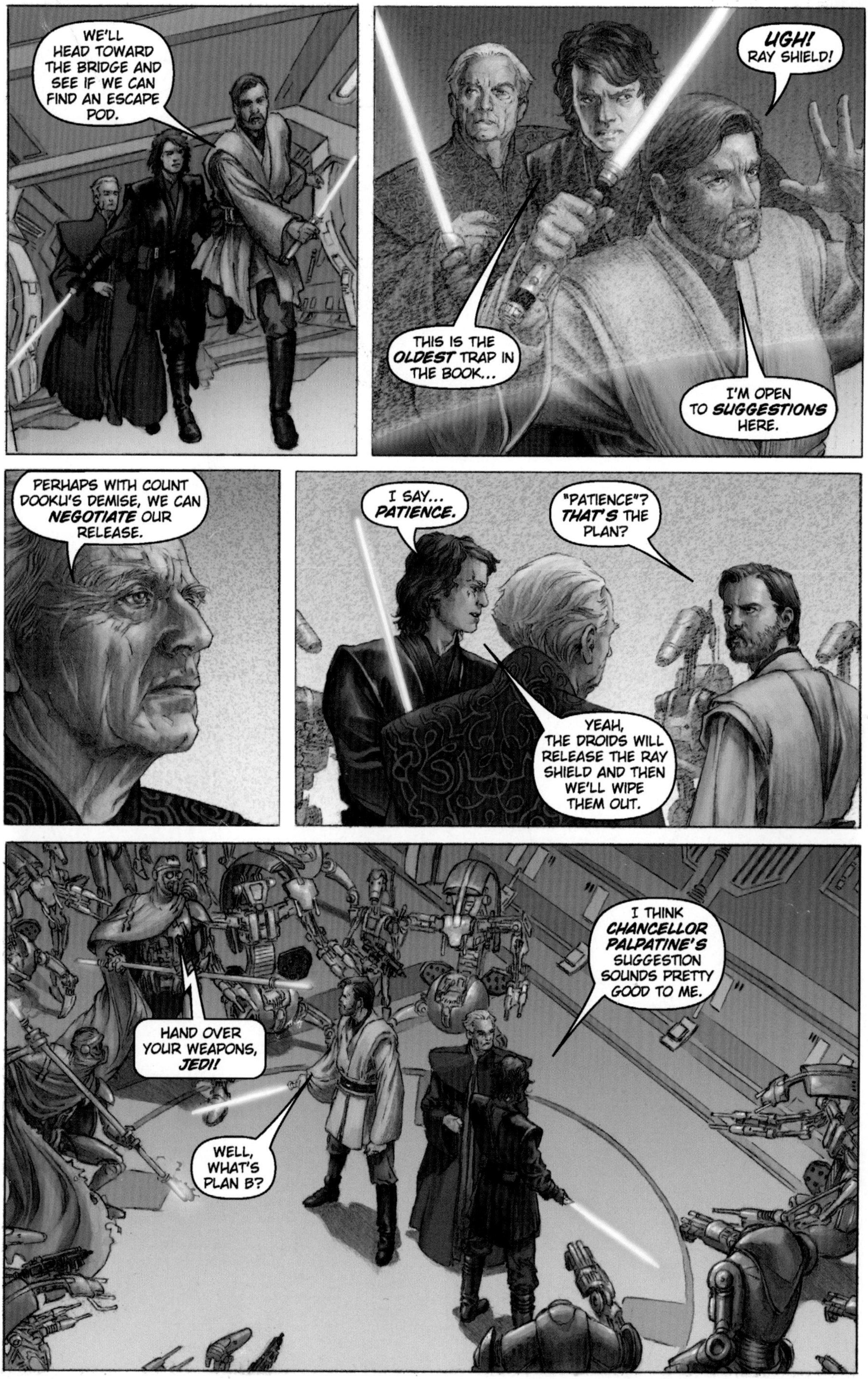
WE'LL HEAD TOWARD THE BRIDGE AND SEE IF WE CAN FIND AN ESCAPE POD.
UGH! RAY SHIELD!
THIS IS THE OLDEST TRAP IN THE BOOK...
I'M OPEN TO SUGGESTIONS HERE.
PERHAPS WITH COUNT DOOKU'S DEMISE, WE CAN NEGOTIATE OUR RELEASE.
I SAY... PATIENCE.
"PATIENCE"? THAT'S THE PLAN?
YEAH, THE DROIDS WILL RELEASE THE RAY SHIELD AND THEN WE'LL WIPE THEM OUT.
HAND OVER YOUR WEAPONS, JEDI!
I THINK CHANCELLOR PALPATINE'S SUGGESTION SOUNDS PRETTY GOOD TO ME.
WELL, WHAT'S PLAN B?

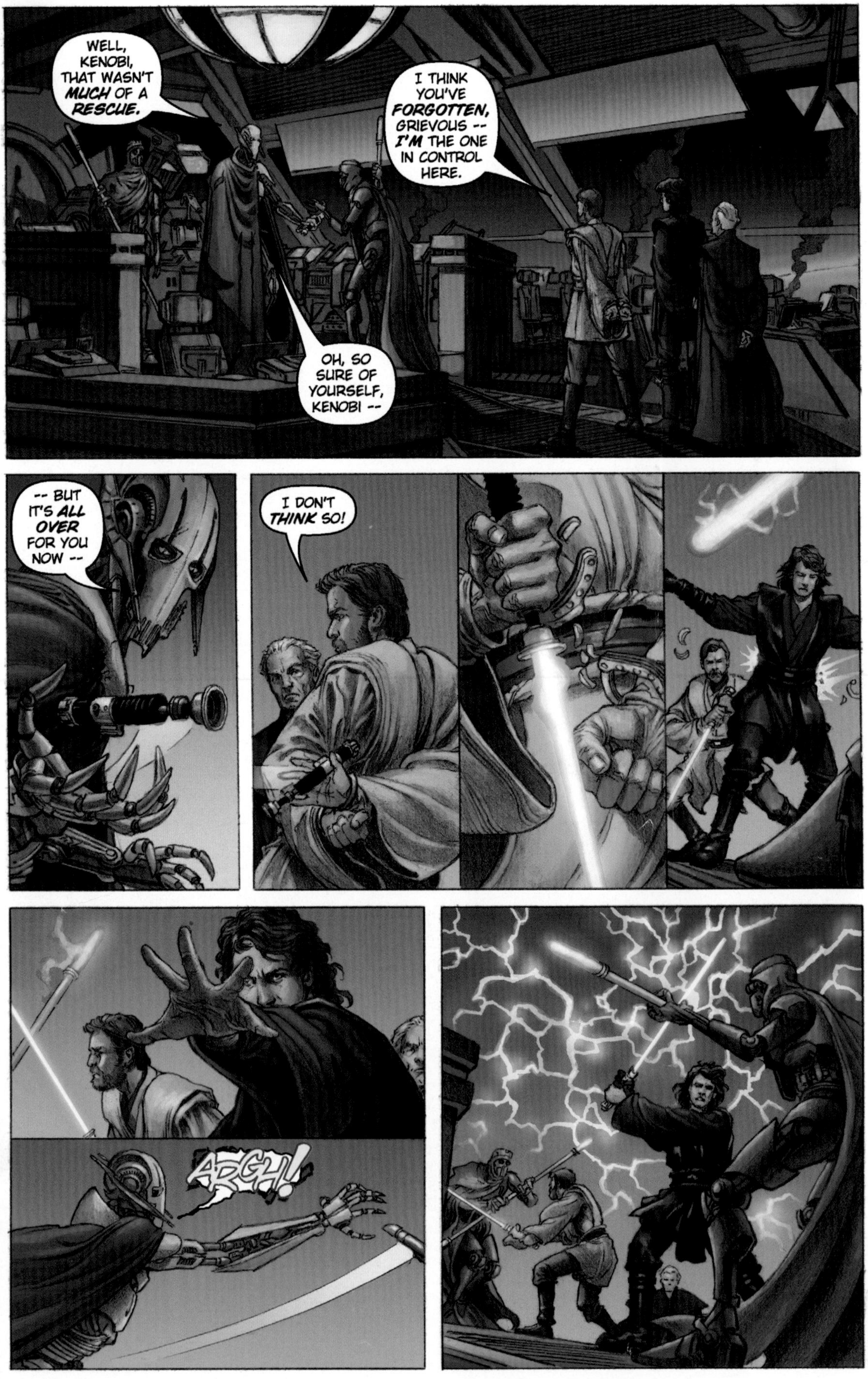
WELL, KENOBI, THAT WASN'T MUCH OF A RESCUE.
I THINK YOU'VE FORGOTTEN, GRIEVOUS -- I'M THE ONE IN CONTROL HERE.
OH, SO SURE OF YOURSELF, KENOBI --
-- BUT IT'S ALL OVER FOR YOU NOW --
I DON'T THINK SO!
ARGH!

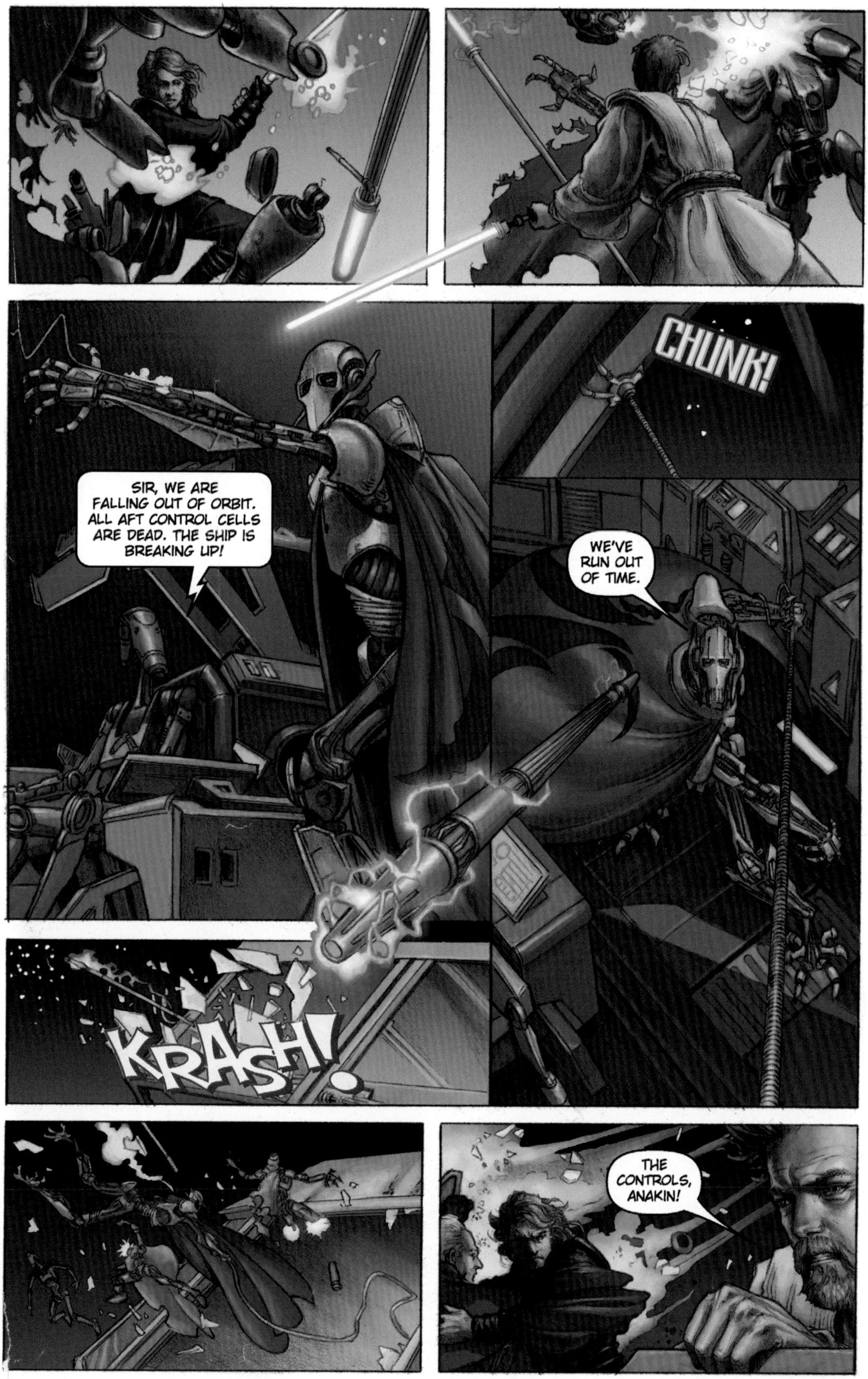
SIR, WE ARE FALLING OUT OF ORBIT. ALL AFT CONTROL CELLS ARE DEAD. THE SHIP IS BREAKING UP!
CHUNK!
WE'VE RUN OUT OF TIME.
KRASH!
THE CONTROLS, ANAKIN!

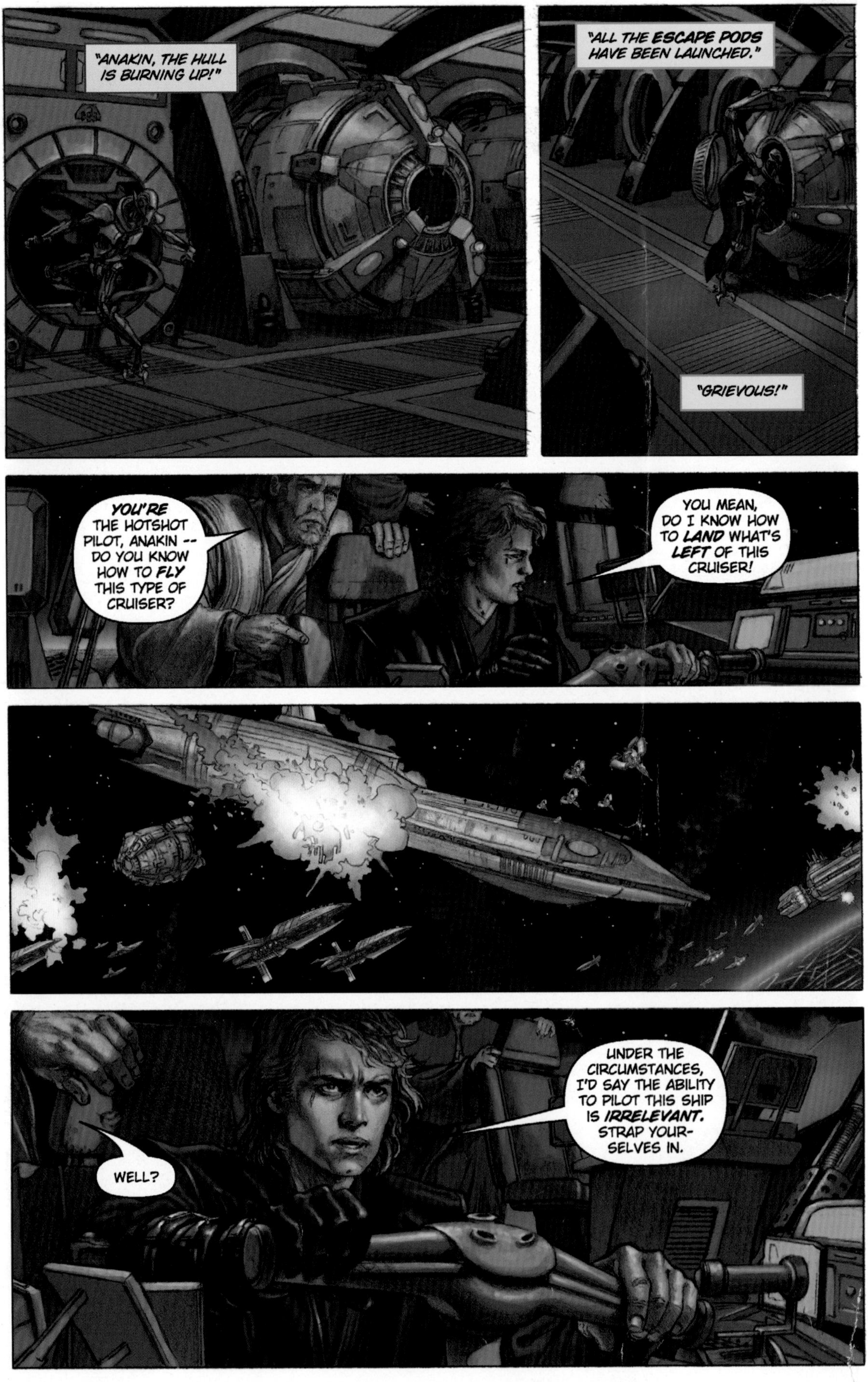
"ANAKIN, THE HULL IS BURNING UP!"
"ALL THE ESCAPE PODS HAVE BEEN LAUNCHED."
"GRIEVOUS!"
YOU'RE THE HOTSHOT PILOT, ANAKIN -- DO YOU KNOW HOW TO FLY THIS TYPE OF CRUISER?
YOU MEAN, DO I KNOW HOW TO LAND WHAT'S LEFT OF THIS CRUISER!
UNDER THE CIRCUMSTANCES, I'D SAY THE ABILITY TO PILOT THIS SHIP IS IRRELEVANT. STRAP YOURSELVES IN.
WELL?

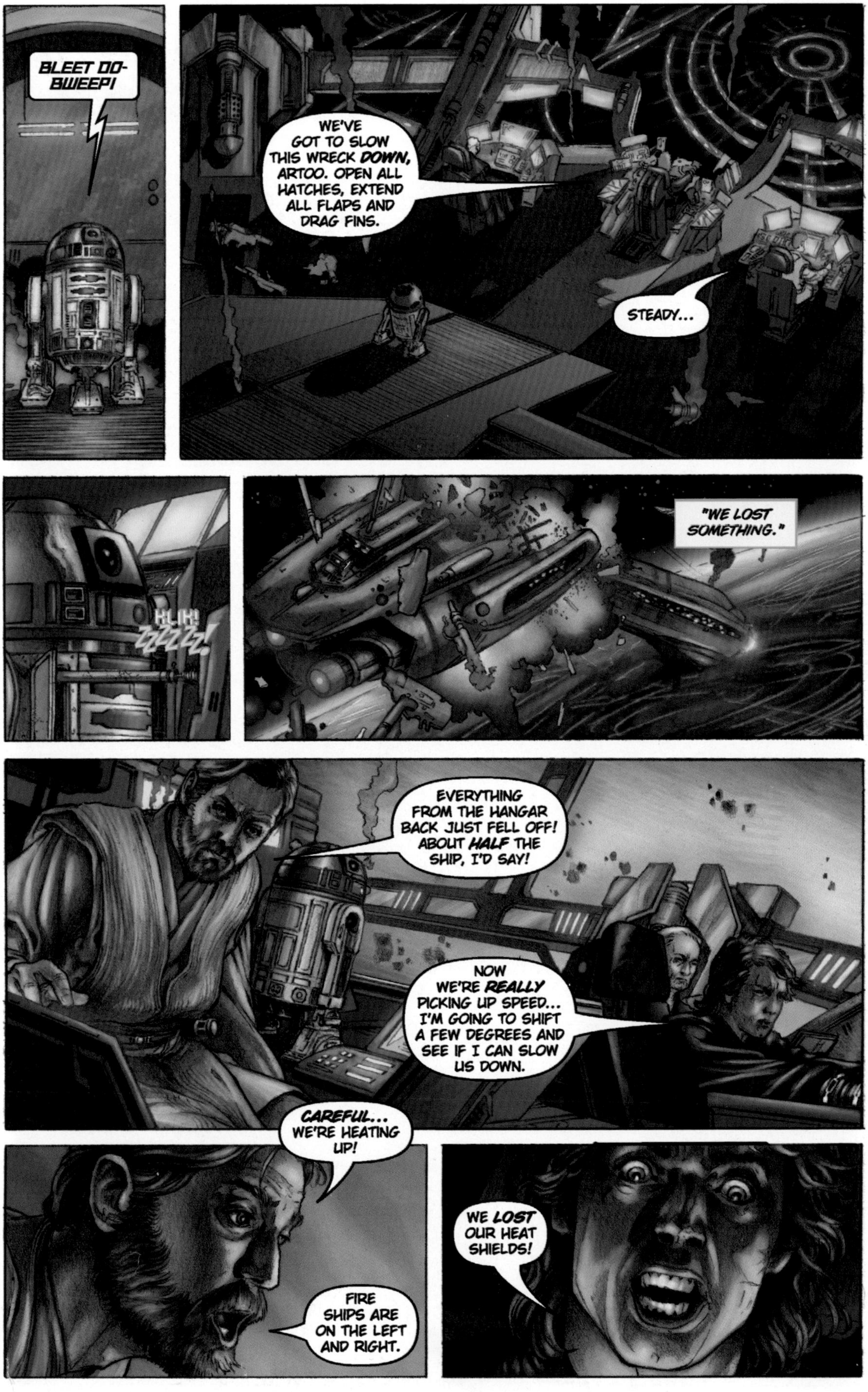
BLEET DO-BWEEP!
WE'VE GOT TO SLOW THIS WRECK DOWN, ARTOO. OPEN ALL HATCHES, EXTEND ALL FLAPS AND DRAG FINS.
STEADY...
KLIK! ZZZZZZ!
"WE LOST SOMETHING."
EVERYTHING FROM THE HANGAR BACK JUST FELL OFF! ABOUT HALF THE SHIP, I'D SAY!
NOW WE'RE REALLY PICKING UP SPEED... I'M GOING TO SHIFT A FEW DEGREES AND SEE IF I CAN SLOW US DOWN.
CAREFUL... WE'RE HEATING UP!
FIRE SHIPS ARE ON THE LEFT AND RIGHT.
WE LOST OUR HEAT SHIELDS!

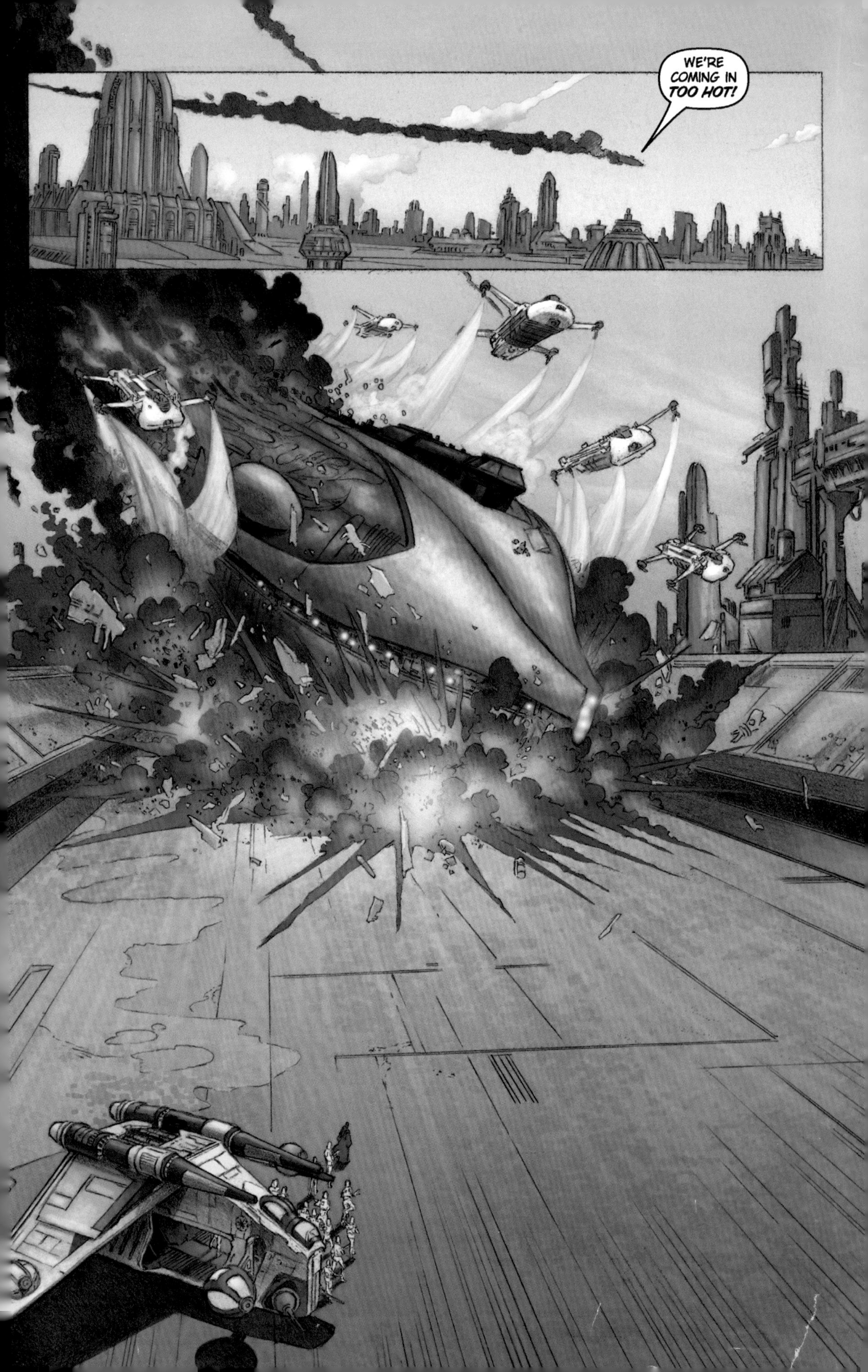
WE'RE COMING IN TOO HOT!

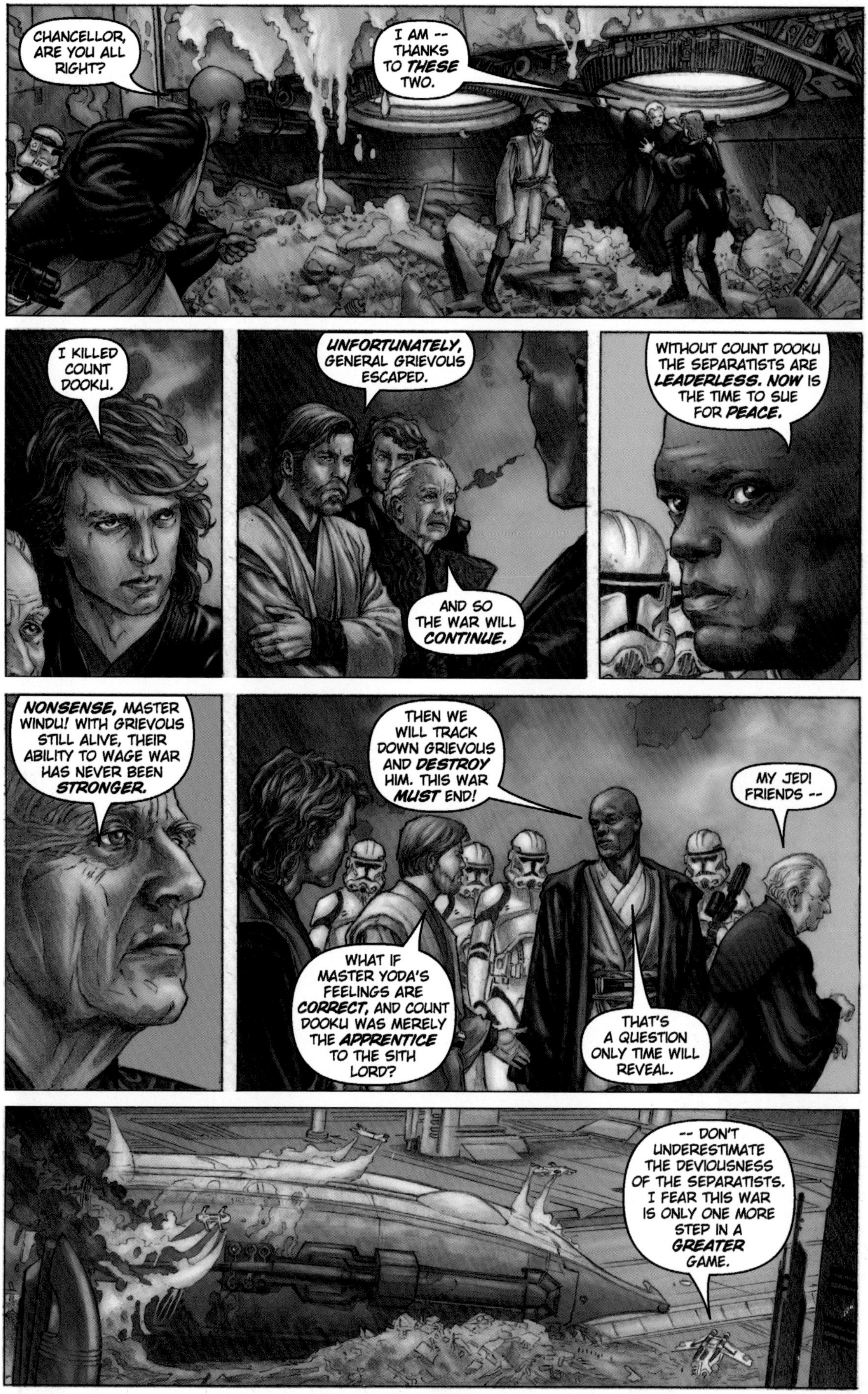
CHANCELLOR, ARE YOU ALL RIGHT?
I AM -- THANKS TO THESE TWO.
I KILLED COUNT DOOKU.
UNFORTUNATELY, GENERAL GRIEVOUS ESCAPED.
AND SO THE WAR WILL CONTINUE.
WITHOUT COUNT DOOKU THE SEPARATISTS ARE LEADERLESS. NOW IS THE TIME TO SUE FOR PEACE.
NONSENSE, MASTER WINDU! WITH GRIEVOUS STILL ALIVE, THEIR ABILITY TO WAGE WAR HAS NEVER BEEN STRONGER.
THEN WE WILL TRACK DOWN GRIEVOUS AND DESTROY HIM. THIS WAR MUST END!
MY JEDI FRIENDS --
WHAT IF MASTER YODA'S FEELINGS ARE CORRECT, AND COUNT DOOKU WAS MERELY THE APPRENTICE TO THE SITH LORD?
THAT'S A QUESTION ONLY TIME WILL REVEAL.
-- DON'T UNDERESTIMATE THE DEVIOUSNESS OF THE SEPARATISTS. I FEAR THIS WAR IS ONLY ONE MORE STEP IN A GREATER GAME.

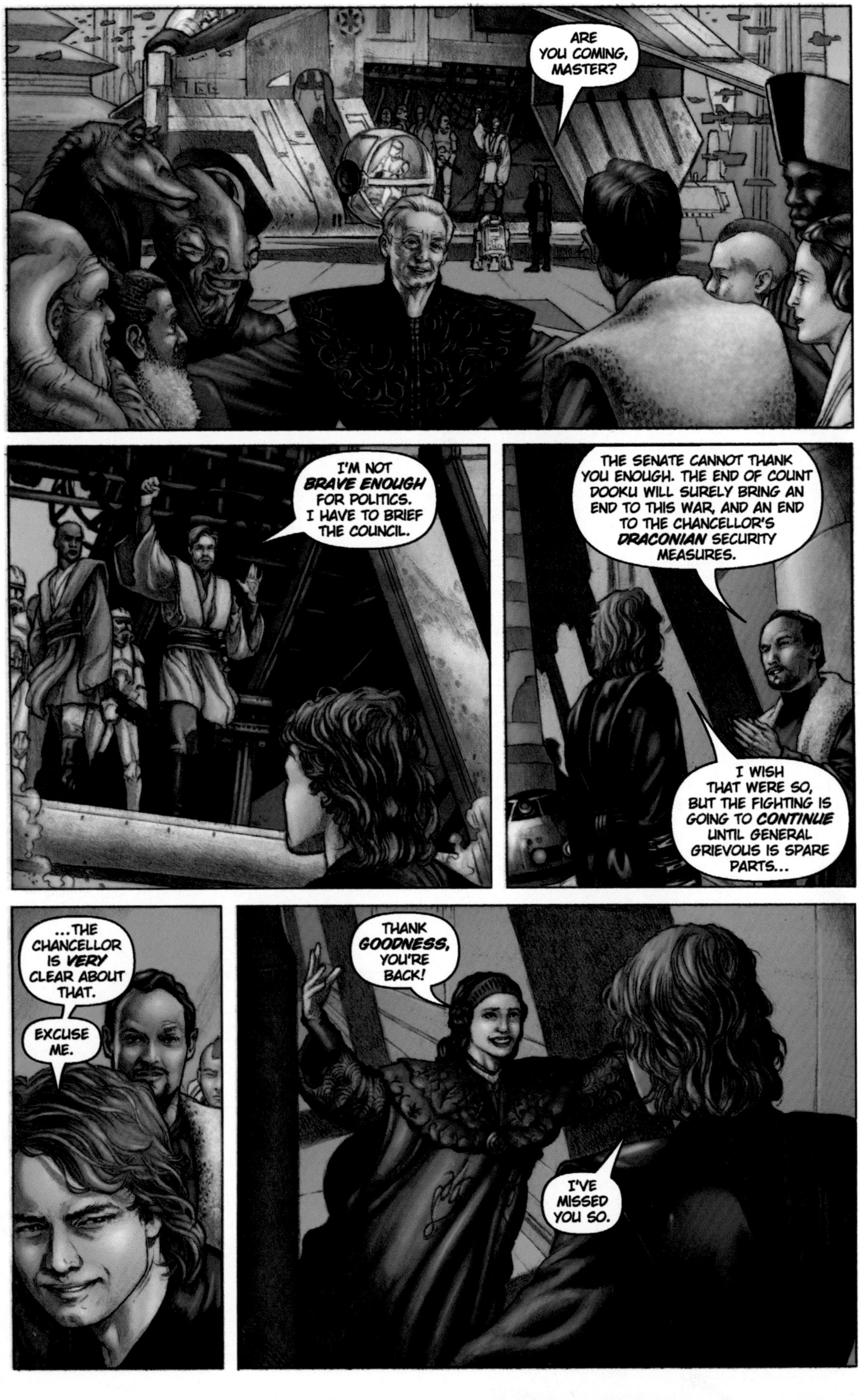
ARE YOU COMING, MASTER?
I'M NOT *BRAVE ENOUGH* FOR POLITICS. I HAVE TO BRIEF THE COUNCIL.
THE SENATE CANNOT THANK YOU ENOUGH. THE END OF COUNT DOOKU WILL SURELY BRING AN END TO THIS WAR, AND AN END TO THE CHANCELLOR'S *DRACONIAN* SECURITY MEASURES.
I WISH THAT WERE SO, BUT THE FIGHTING IS GOING TO *CONTINUE* UNTIL GENERAL GRIEVOUS IS SPARE PARTS...
...THE CHANCELLOR IS *VERY* CLEAR ABOUT THAT.
EXCUSE ME.
THANK *GOODNESS,* YOU'RE BACK!
I'VE MISSED YOU SO.

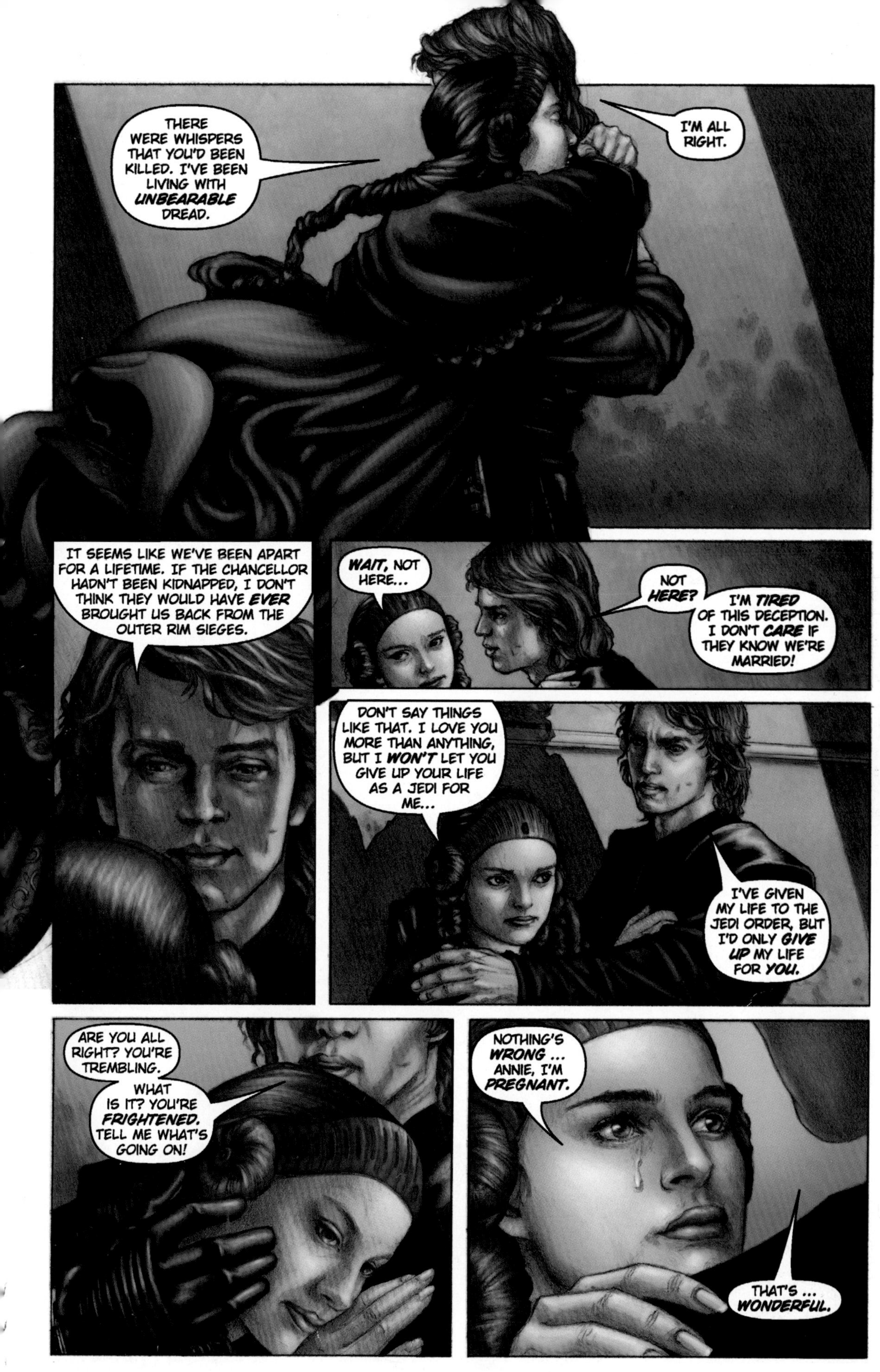
THERE WERE WHISPERS THAT YOU'D BEEN KILLED. I'VE BEEN LIVING WITH UNBEARABLE DREAD.
I'M ALL RIGHT.
IT SEEMS LIKE WE'VE BEEN APART FOR A LIFETIME. IF THE CHANCELLOR HADN'T BEEN KIDNAPPED, I DON'T THINK THEY WOULD HAVE EVER BROUGHT US BACK FROM THE OUTER RIM SIEGES.
WAIT, NOT HERE...
NOT HERE?
I'M TIRED OF THIS DECEPTION. I DON'T CARE IF THEY KNOW WE'RE MARRIED!
DON'T SAY THINGS LIKE THAT. I LOVE YOU MORE THAN ANYTHING, BUT I WON'T LET YOU GIVE UP YOUR LIFE AS A JEDI FOR ME...
I'VE GIVEN MY LIFE TO THE JEDI ORDER, BUT I'D ONLY GIVE UP MY LIFE FOR YOU.
ARE YOU ALL RIGHT? YOU'RE TREMBLING.
WHAT IS IT? YOU'RE FRIGHTENED. TELL ME WHAT'S GOING ON!
NOTHING'S WRONG ... ANNIE, I'M PREGNANT.
THAT'S ... WONDERFUL.

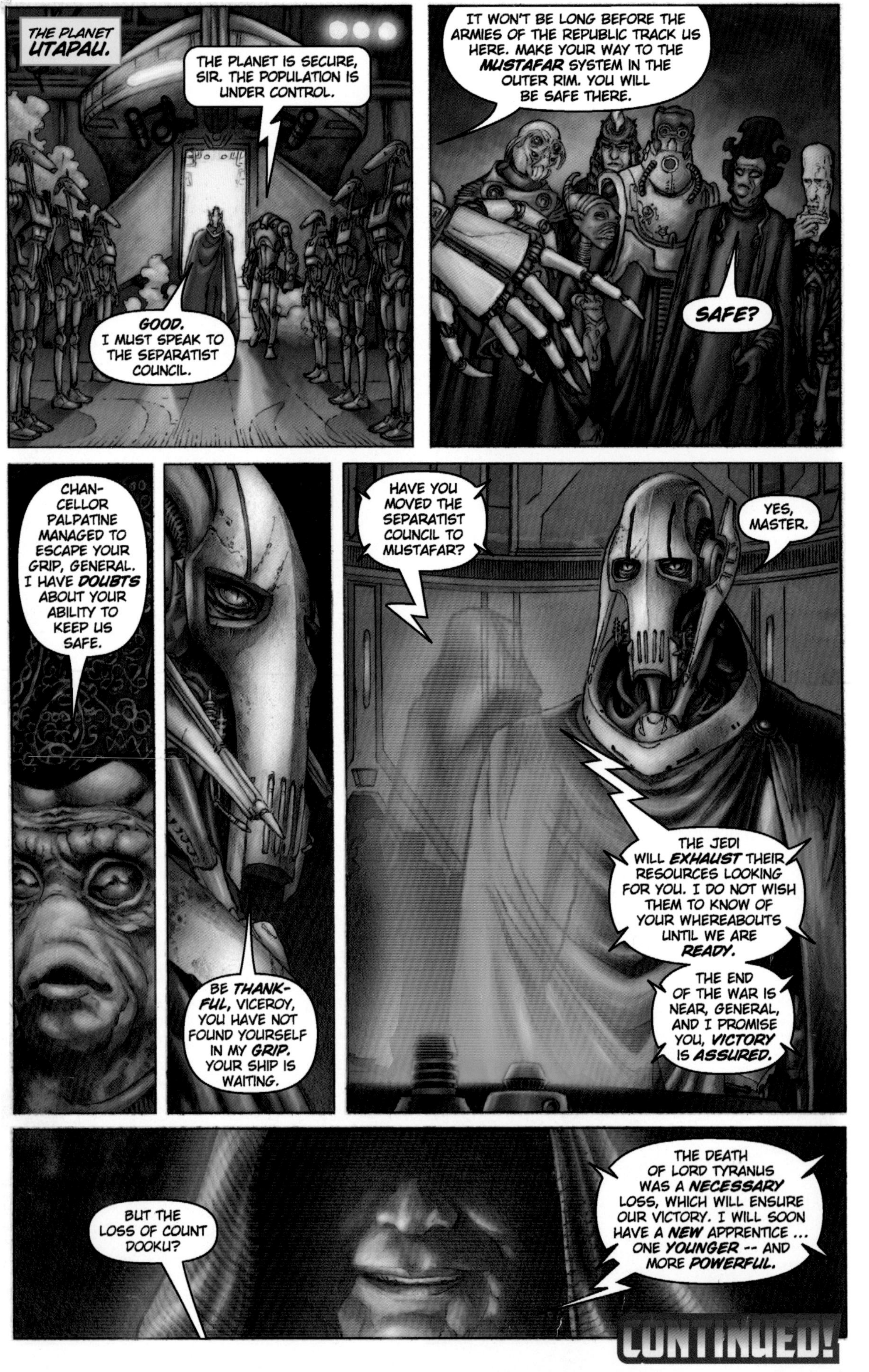
THE PLANET UTAPAU.
THE PLANET IS SECURE, SIR. THE POPULATION IS UNDER CONTROL.
GOOD. I MUST SPEAK TO THE SEPARATIST COUNCIL.
IT WON'T BE LONG BEFORE THE ARMIES OF THE REPUBLIC TRACK US HERE. MAKE YOUR WAY TO THE MUSTAFAR SYSTEM IN THE OUTER RIM. YOU WILL BE SAFE THERE.
SAFE?
CHAN-CELLOR PALPATINE MANAGED TO ESCAPE YOUR GRIP, GENERAL. I HAVE DOUBTS ABOUT YOUR ABILITY TO KEEP US SAFE.
BE THANK-FUL, VICEROY, YOU HAVE NOT FOUND YOURSELF IN MY GRIP. YOUR SHIP IS WAITING.
HAVE YOU MOVED THE SEPARATIST COUNCIL TO MUSTAFAR?
YES, MASTER.
THE JEDI WILL EXHAUST THEIR RESOURCES LOOKING FOR YOU. I DO NOT WISH THEM TO KNOW OF YOUR WHEREABOUTS UNTIL WE ARE READY.
THE END OF THE WAR IS NEAR, GENERAL, AND I PROMISE YOU, VICTORY IS ASSURED.
BUT THE LOSS OF COUNT DOOKU?
THE DEATH OF LORD TYRANUS WAS A NECESSARY LOSS, WHICH WILL ENSURE OUR VICTORY. I WILL SOON HAVE A NEW APPRENTICE ... ONE YOUNGER -- AND MORE POWERFUL.
CONTINUED!